The Phoenix

An Alumière Sisters' Adventure

Morgan Delaney

Published by Morgan Delaney

www.morgandelaney.info

Contact: morgan@morgandelaney.info

Edited by Claire Rushbrook

Cover design by Celin Graphics

The Phoenix/ Morgan Delaney. —1st ed.

Print ISBN 978-3-98566-000-1

E-book ISBN 978-3-98566-001-8

Contents

For Nadine,
for the next four centuries and beyond!

Welcome to Hawkinge-By-Hythe!

To make the most of your stay, please note that the spelling is UK English, the measurements are imperial and the temperatures are in degrees Celsius.

Any mention of "football" refers to soccer, and any beer you order will be warm.

Chapter 1

The Bowling Over Of Sniffacre

"CALL ME JENNET," said Mrs Sniffacre, hefting her basket, laden with packets of assorted animal feed. Then she fainted.

She had stepped from Mr Carde's shop into a tide of swarming rats. It was almost like they had been waiting for her. One moment she had been chatting, the next the town was awash with vermin. Their fur – filthy black and matted brown – flowed over her feet and rubbed her ankles through her stockings. She was a country woman, born and bred, and didn't scare easily, but there were hundreds of rats, scritching their paws down the cobblestones of High Street. From the door of Carde's Chandlery to the whitewashed wall of the pub across the road, seethed a bubbling stream of racing furry bodies and pink worm-like tails. Their claws scraped stone and boiled around Mrs Sniffacre's legs, splashing through the blue, metal dog bowl outside Carde's door. Her feet had disappeared under their feverish weight. They clambered over each other and under her skirts. A wet nose touched the inside of her leg and that's what did it. It could have been a kiss. She swooned.

Luckily, the old widow swooned into Jeb's strong, smooth arms. He had opened the door to let her through with her purchases and stood transfixed by the dank wash of rodents outside. He was barely aware of her even as he caught her, while rats poured past.

"Close the door!" shouted Mr Carde from behind the counter. But the tide had passed before Jeb could stir himself. Screams preceded the rats as they barrelled down the High Street. Mr Carde hurried to the door in time to see a yellow pellet of rock sulphur roll to a halt on the now otherwise deserted street. He added the rock sulphur as a service, free of charge to his customers. Left in a dog's water bowl, it cooled the animals' blood and rendered them docile and amenable. Owners – or rather, their dogs – could sample the marvellous mineral from the blue water bowl outside his door. Packets were available for purchase upon request. It did not, however, appear to appeal to rats.

Jeb assisted Mrs Sniffacre – Jennet – to a chair behind the counter. Mr Carde's chandlery sold all manner of grains, brans, mashes and other animal feed. It also supplied the animals which ate it, in case a potential customer should try to argue that he did not need animal feed, for want of an animal to feed it to. The bitter ammoniac tang of chicken droppings mixed powerfully with the fruity, yet dusty aroma of grains and ageing potatoes. Smelling salts were therefore unnecessary. Mrs Sniffacre came to and found herself looking straight into Jeb's blue eyes. She forced herself to get up, but held onto his thick upper arm. For some reason, this close to Jeb, she still felt faint.

"Their little noses!" she said. "All twitching. It was too much. It's a plague."

"Just the heat," said Mr Carde, careful of the fact that a man who sold animal feed cannot afford to get worked up about an overabundance of animals. He was also thankful that his shop had been spared, despite being a prime potential target. And there may well have been something in it. The summer had been an absolute scorcher, it was reasonable to assume that the heatwave might be affecting the rats. This had not been the first time they had been sighted.

"You're okay?" asked Jeb.

Mrs Sniffacre looked herself over in wonder. "I am," she said. "Not a mark. Thanks to you, Jeb!" She squeezed his arm.

"No problem," said Jeb. "It looks like they're gone."

She shuddered. "You won't make me go out there by myself, will you?"

"Jeb," said Mr Carde. "Would you accompany Mrs Sniffacre home?" She was a good customer. Especially during the last few weeks, though he wasn't aware that she had increased her livestock.

He put that down to the heat, too. Several of his lady customers had recently upped their orders, and he congratulated himself on his business acumen. He had engaged the barrel-chested and good-natured Jeb right about the time his business had picked up. Speaking personally, he found Jeb to be sorely lacking in sensible conversation and the way he flicked back his thick black hair could not be described as anything other than foppish. But he was undeniably popular with Mrs Mudge, Mrs Sniffacre and Mrs Deverill, in addition to the Misses Tinfeld and Cornigan, among others.

"I need a drink," said Mrs Sniffacre. "And so do you!" she informed Jeb as she marched him out. Jeb cast an apologetic glance back at Mr Carde.

Business was booming, he had been spared the rats, and he personally enjoyed the heat, but still... Not once in over thirty years had he been invited for a drink. He picked a pinch of bran from a trough and chewed it as he stared after Jeb and Mrs Sniffacre as they disappeared into the lounge bar of The Damme Billett across the road, Jeb carrying Mrs Sniffacre's laden basket easily on one arm. Mr Carde tried flicking his hair back as he turned and returned inside. Perhaps he would let it grow a little longer, once the heat had passed.

The Bowling Over Of Sniffacre, as the incident became known, marked the day when the weeds of panic started to sprout in Hawkinge-By-Hythe. Farmers had reported sightings throughout the countryside for several weeks: rats swarming before dashing arrow straight towards some destination of utmost rodent importance. Nobody knew where they were going, or if they did, they weren't saying. The rats had startled farmers as they poured across the roads and laneways from one field to another. They had spooked cows and sheep as they scuttled through grazing fields, but the trail soon went cold. Speculation was rife, but the town council had put the problem aside as being basically agricultural. Now, however, the rats had invaded the town, and it was still only the end of July, with the heatwave set to continue. The thought that the sun-crazed rats might soon also become a feature of the town, and that the cream of Hawkinge-By-Hythe's society would have to get through, at a minimum, the entirety of August before a respite could be expected was too much to bear. Especially, as Mr Oaten pointed out, as there was every reason to expect things would certainly only get worse: it was likely that the rats would become even more aggressive once the crops were harvested, and there was neither food nor shelter for them to be had in the countryside.

Everyone reacted according to their character. Mr Carde had decided it was the presence of rock sulphur which had saved his shop and was quick to point out this supplementary benefit. Not only did it soothe dogs and other desirable animals, but was spectacularly efficacious as a deterrent of undesirable ones. Just as vampires shun garlic, so did rats shun rock sulphur, avoiding it whether procured in its standard- or economy-sized bags, both of which were available at very competitive prices. Jeb delivered sacks of the stuff all around town. Mrs Mudge was managing to get through two large bags per week, never tiring of hearing Jeb recount how he had barely escaped being eaten alive, though less interested in how he had saved Mrs Sniffacre, whose brush with the infinite had surely been even closer. Reverend Gresstart was quick to denounce the behaviour of the rats as immoral. His denunciation was of limited practical utility, but it did the townsfolk good to hear that the rats would get what was coming to them, as soon as the Lord showed up. Alderman Fawsick convened the council to discuss a plan, but was unable to decide on one course of action over another once his suggestion that the Alumière sisters be contacted was shot down by the reverend. Mrs Delbing disseminated folk remedies based on the usually unhygienic things that her grandmother used to do. Those of the town's inhabitants who had relatives elsewhere remembered that it had been far too long since they had visited them, and the eternally absent Muirs, who had been expected to finally return to the town after an extended stay in Switzerland, leapfrogged it completely and made themselves comfortable with a Lord Something or Other in Scotland instead. They were not sorely missed, but poor communication of their change in plans led to initial rumours that they returned and been eaten by the rats shortly thereafter. Dogs and cats, who had been enjoying the freedom of the countryside, were required to stay indoors to avoid becoming victims of the rat poison, which was strewn everywhere.

And a second, more insidious rumour started to gain traction in the town: The rats were Dame Holte's revenge.

Victoria Alumière had come across Dame Holte many times during her researches into the town's legends: she had been hanged as a witch almost exactly four hundred years ago. Local legend ascribed her various powers, both before and after her death. She had been hung from the oak tree in Bagnell's field before being buried between its roots, from which she occasionally escaped to turn milk, glare at drunks or gloatingly pass on bad news from the netherworld. Digging into the facts, it seemed likely that, if nothing else, she had survived rather too many wealthy husbands for her own good. And the reverend's stentorian sermons against the rats only strengthened everyone's conviction that the evil old witch must be behind matters.

The Alumière sisters rather preferred to search for a more rational explanation. They were the proprietors of Hawkinge-by-Hythe's apothecary shop and intensely interested in anything scientifically unusual. This surely qualified. They were new to the town, having arrived recently from abroad. They had no accent, but it was assumed they came from France. Their manner was certainly what one would expect from those used to mixing in Paris's intellectual and artistic circles. They told it like it was. Together with their involvement in a handful of local incidents, which had escalated to an unfortunate degree, this was cause for them to be regarded with a certain wariness. Their striking similarity to one another – which is to say that Victoria, Gertrude and Colette Alumière looked absolutely identical – was another, though it didn't appear to bother the sisters. In fact, they exacerbated the issue by dressing similarly – which is to say, identically – too. It was practically a uniform, one chosen to perfectly marry the requirements of comfort, ease of movement, and style. Black culottes, over steel-capped black lace-up boots. Black ruffled blouses buttoned to the necks. And black high-crowned pork pie hats with rakishly wide brims. Only the differently coloured feathers they affected, one per hat, made it possible for anyone to tell them apart at first glance. Victoria's feather was safflower yellow, Gertrude's was carmine red, while Colette preferred black, which shone silvery powder-grey in sunlight.

They lived in a house on the outskirts of town, which they shared with their two-headed calf, Curly. His friend Chloe Dunsloe, the daughter of his previous owner, regularly visited him. It was from her that the sisters first learned that the local rats were exhibiting unusual behaviour. They were already on the case, therefore, when the alderman decided he would put the matter up to them, regardless of what anyone else thought. He himself had a particular horror of rats. Once, when a child, he had woken to find one on his pillow, twitching its nose at him. Its mouth had been open, revealing thin, curved teeth, perfect for burrowing into flesh. More worrying yet had been his conviction that it had in fact been trying to tell him something urgent.

Meanwhile, the reverend was drafting a most strongly worded letter to The Hawkinge Times. He felt most sorely put upon as he was currently host to a visitor – a tourist, in fact. The first tourist anyone in Hawkinge-By-Hythe could remember – and a foreigner to boot, all the way from Luxembourg.

Chapter 2

The Professor's Trousers And Colette's Buttons

PROFESSOR DE GLUBE was an old friend of the reverend. They had met when they were both studying at the seminary, though de Glube had abandoned his studies before ordination. He had recently arrived in England for a visit and was staying with Gresstart and his wife at the rectory.

"He has changed somewhat in the intervening years," Gresstart explained to his wife after they had shown the professor his room, and before they parted for their own separate bedrooms. "But he was always good to me, and it would be a shame if his holiday were ruined."

"But what does he *want?*" asked Mrs Gresstart. She was taller than her husband and her hair was blacker.

"He's doing research for a book he's writing. Think of him as an archaeologist for religious writings," he said.

Mrs Gresstart thought that a book about a small boring town being overrun by rats would make for a far more exciting read, but kept that to herself. She also thought that it had worked out well for the town that he had arrived at this particular moment. He was a wonderful distraction for the locals, helping to take their minds off their rodent woes. Those trousers!

A certain leeway must, of course, be granted the foreigner in the matter of clothing, but the professor pursued his research attired in the baggiest and flashiest leg coverings that the town had ever seen. In a large city such as London, they might not have attracted much comment, being a sober Egyptian blue with discreet ochre pinstripes. But Hawkinge-By-Hythians were staunch believers in the holy trinity of black, brown and grey for trousers, and their world was being rocked by his unorthodox slacks. He seemed oblivious of the effect of his attire on the normally sleepy town, even to the extent of occasionally handing out sixpences to the throng of local children who followed him wherever he went, unaware that he was the object of their ridicule. As long as he was not accompanied by the reverend, naturally. The reverend regularly condemned them to eternal hellfire for such sins as not combing their hair; running on a Sunday; or sniffing while he was talking. They wouldn't dare mock one of his friends in his presence. But children are naturally curious creatures and these eager minds were keen to discover whether the professor had bought the trousers, or was being paid to take them away, and if he would be amenable to wearing them at night to supplement the town's inadequate street lighting, which did not blaze half as bright.

The professor meanwhile was indeed on a research mission, scouring local monuments, churches and graveyards for miles around. He found the children a pleasant and interested audience to whom he was able to entrust his theories and ideas. The children, for their part, were a most willing audience. They had spent their entire brief lives in Hawkinge-By-Hythe and, for them, his accent was possibly the only thing that could top his trousers. As they often explained to each other, "et wash ze foonniest ting dey 'ad ever 'urd". There was a minor school of thought in the town that held the professor responsible for the rats' behaviour. This school was unable to gain much traction, however, as it was itself split into two further factions: those who thought that his trousers were so outrageous that he was unconsciously exciting the rats, which felt compelled to investigate the prismatic fabric; and those who felt that the rats were so terrified of being blinded by the colourful trews that they fled whenever he approached. As the professor spent most of his days tramping the surrounding countryside, either theory was plausible: that the rats gathered to flee towards, or away from, the professor and his vibrant and voluminous pantaloons.

So far there was nothing to indicate that the professor had been molested by the rats. Each evening he returned to Hawkinge-By-Hythe with his notebook in hand and a satisfied smile on his face, trailing a tired straggle of children still enquiring politely, if he intended to return the rainbow when he had finished wearing it.

As Alderman Fawsick arrived at the house belonging to the Alumière sisters and rang the bell, memories of the last time he had visited rose in his memory, so that he was relieved rather than insulted when Gertrude, distracted by her own research on the topic, neglected to invite him in, after hearing him out. She closed the front door in his face. He glanced around for the two-headed Curly, then scrambled back to his blue Wolseley where the town's constable, who doubled as bodyguard and driver, sped them homewards. The alderman breathed a sigh of relief. He found the ladies eminently capable, but indubitably formidable, while the looks that Curly gave him whenever they "met" could only be described as inscrutable.

"The alderman," said Gertrude as she returned to her sisters. They had marked out all the reported rat sightings on a large map in their second sitting room, which Colette referred to as their War Room. Colette was also acting as Paymaster to a select cadre of the town's children, who reported back on the professor's travels around the countryside. This too they documented on the map. As the sisters suspected, there did not appear to be any overlap between the two items. On the other hand, his journeys were interesting in their own right.

The map was more complete for the professor than for the rats as he was hard to lose sight of, while the rats moved fast, then disappeared. Their movements were usually just brief dashed lines on the map where sightings had been confirmed. If they were to extend the lines by pencil, however, it provided them with an interesting clue: if they were to assume that the rats were truly moving in a straight line, rather than zig-zagging, then they appeared to be heading towards a particular field to the west of Hawking-By-Hythe. Further research suggested that this was the site of a local ley line.

Apart from the empirical confirmation that this was indeed where the rats were going, a number of further questions therefore remained open. What was behind the rats' sudden interest in ley lines, an idea which was still new to the human scientific community? Since when had rats been aware of the theory? Given that their interest in ley lines was genuine, what was it about this particular one that excited them so intensely and in such numbers? But the biggest question related to something else. West of the town, the countryside belonged for the most part to the Kelby family. The Kelbys were farmers with deep roots in the area. The current Kelby had a keen eye for a bargain, but was well-liked in the community, too. He employed quite a few of the nearby families, many of them throughout the year. It seemed odd that neither he nor his labourers had noticed swarms of rats descending on his fields, especially this close to harvest time, when every farmer lived on tenterhooks, lest something go wrong at the last moment. The sisters decided to pay him a visit.

Kelby was not at the farmhouse when they called. His wife informed them he could be found either in or near the Turner field. The one at the top of the gentle hill, one of the highest that he owned. The one, each Alumière silently noted to herself, that so intrigued the local rats.

"Ideally we should wait for him," said Victoria, when they arrived at Turner's field. But she was already examining the ground. Rat droppings were scattered everywhere. "Oh, they've been here many times."

Gertrude climbed onto the stile to get a better view of the field, but the wheat was too high to allow her to see much other than Kelby hurrying towards them.

Colette unpacked her camera to take photos of the scene.

"What are you doing with the rats, Kelby?" asked Gertrude.

His face turned white, and he shot a look around. There was nobody close by. "How did you find out?"

"Someone squealed," said Colette.

Kelby, it turned out, knew little about the rats, other than that they had been sighted on numerous occasions. He had seen them himself on two separate occasions. They came, they rushed around his field, then they disappeared. "It sounds like the ocean, when they run," he said. He was worried. Even if the rats didn't destroy his crop, he might well find himself unable to sell it, if people found out it was somehow behind the trouble with the rats.

"It's your own fault," said Gertrude. "You should have told us." She waved a finger. "Next time," she said, with no need to elaborate. He nodded gratefully.

Gertrude was a hard woman to lie to, and they were satisfied that he was telling the truth. He was obviously relieved at being able to talk about it.

"Who are the Turners?" asked Gertrude, referring to the name his wife had used to identify the field for them.

Kelby cleared his throat. "We bought the land from him. My family from his family."

Gertrude waited.

"Just farmers, they've long gone." He examined a rat dropping close to the front of his boot, then kicked it. "Dame Holte was a Turner before she married."

The sisters took samples of the droppings, of the soil, the wheat and the hedges and recorded their impressions. They made plans for a number of stake-outs, aware that they would need luck as they had no schedule with which they could work. Kelby volunteered to help. He and his son Andrew would organise someone to keep an eye on the field at all times and report back. The rats were an open secret. The men and women who worked his fields knew all about them, but had been silent on the matter out of loyalty.

Once they had made the arrangements and collected the on-site evidence, they returned to the War Room to synthesise their findings. Which did not amount to much. Victoria volunteered to research local histories and the parish records for information, in case the past held a clue as to what was happening. She was glad to get out of the house. Colette and Gertrude remained in the War Room, writing up notes. And fighting.

It was because of the camera. Gertrude had sniffed when Colette had purchased the Bakelite Purma Special. Gertrude had nothing against cameras, they could be very useful, but the small handheld gadget was to her mind a vanity toy, not a serious instrument. Her suspicions that Colette was becoming 'unserious' deepened when she had caught her in conversation with Jeb. She was supposed to be buying feed for Curly. Instead, she had been draped over the counter, leaning in to the big lummox, proudly showing off her toy. Gertrude knew full well that Jeb was a handsome creature, if not to her taste, and was upset that Colette would want to waste herself on such a man. Furthermore, despite the heatwave, both Gertrude and Victoria kept their blouses buttoned up to the top, while Colette had taken to leaving her top button undone. Gertrude saw this as a lack of solidarity. She was proud of herself and her sisters and all they had accomplished, both individually and as a whole. She did not accept Colette's argument that it was silly to suffer through a heatwave buttoned up and be-hatted.

It was a matter of principle, as far as Gertrude was concerned. Jeb had turned Colette's head, and she was flaunting herself.

As far as Colette, on the other hand, was concerned, it was:

(a) none of Gertrude's business what she, Colette, did with her buttons;

(b) nobody's business but her own, what she, Colette, spent her money on and her, Gertrude's, own silly fault, if she was unable to appreciate the strides technology was making. Other people, such as to take an example at random, Jeb could see the possibilities that a portable camera offered and understood that it was not a toy.

"A-ha!" said Gertrude. "I knew it, he only –"

(c) none of Gertrude's damned business who she showed her camera to and;

(d) up to her, Colette, to decide with whom she spent her time and how she looked while she did it.

"He has half the town's women chasing after him, he –"

Furthermore:

(e) Gertrude might have been the oldest of the three sisters, but only by a matter of minutes, and that didn't give her the right to tell her, Colette, what she could do.

The summer was wearing on everyone and Victoria decided to:

(f) let them work it out for themselves. In the meantime, the library was cool and the parish records were interesting and informative.

The summer was very hot.

Chapter 3

A Picnic And Not A Bite Taken

"IT COULD GO ON LIKE THIS FOREVER," said Colette.

"Lovely," said Victoria.

They had finished their picnic lunch and now lay on a striped blanket, under the shade of the oak tree in Bagnell's field. A breeze took the edge off the heat. They weren't the only ones who had had the idea on the Sunday before the Summer Bank holiday. The field was stuffed to bursting with locals, enjoying the view and the air. Gertrude ignored them all, though she kept an eye on Jeb from under her red-feathered pork-pie hat. She would normally unwind enough to take it off on such a day, but Colette's top button was still undone, and she was determined to make a stand. Jeb and Colette had spent an increasing amount of evenings together. Far too many for Gertrude's liking. Now he sat at the lower end of the field with several friends, attempting simultaneously to keep a low profile and catch Colette's eye. His efforts were futile. He was clearly already the centre of a lot of female attention and that would have to be enough for him as Colette did not seem aware of his presence.

The long period of good weather had caused what the Alumière sisters referred to as English Summer Depression: there had been so much nice weather already that the island's population was wracked with anxiety, fearing that each and every new nice day was sure to be the last one, and must be enjoyed to the fullest, no matter the cost. The field hummed with children playing "Seagull," dashing to pick the choicest treats from among the bazaar of rugs belonging to relatives and neighbours. Though there was barely an inch of grass left uncovered in most of the field, the sisters enjoyed relative peace and space, as they had secured their favoured spot on the swelling roots of the oak tree. This was because it was the infamous Hanging Tree. Back when it was the done thing, Dame Holte, along with any other local witches, had all dangled from their hangman's ropes among its branches. What was more, Dame Holte was rumoured to be buried underneath it. The reason the oak's roots bulged so, it was said, was that her body continued to grow, even in death. One day she would return, larger than the oak which fed her bones.

Nonsense, of course. The oak's roots bulged because Bagnell did not have very good farmland. And this field had the poorest of the lot, which was why he was so willing to give it over to community events. It had only a thin layer of topsoil over a chalk foundation, and not even the most fat-headed of zealots would have attempted to bury someone there. Nonetheless, the legend lived on and Dame Holte, who had married and allegedly 'witched to death' over a dozen husbands, all of whom had been previously most respectable local dignitaries, grew more notorious with every year that passed.

"You're sweating," said Colette as Gertrude drew a palm across her moist forehead. Despite the breeze, the day was still hot, 26 degrees according to the thermometer, but Gertrude and Victoria held the line, refusing to loosen their top buttons. Victoria would happily have stretched the point, except that she knew how it would upset Gertrude, who merely pursed her lips and sniffed in response to the cheap insult. She certainly was not sweating. Colette had also removed her hat (as had Victoria). It basked in the sun's warmth on the ground beside her. The black feather shimmered grey. If Colette wanted to flirt with Jeb and sunstroke, then let her. She'd find out what he was really worth, when she tried to say hello to him, and he shied back from her red and sunburnt face.

Despite the distance from it, Colette could taste salt from the sea, and indeed her arms glittered with a fine dusting of it, carried on the breeze. If she held her hand over her eyes, she could see the ocean over the heads of a circle of children singing the Hokey Cokey. She ignored Gertrude's sniff, which she correctly interpreted as to mean, "if you were wearing a hat you wouldn't need to do that."

Someone screamed. Then someone else. Then everyone was scrambling and shouting. From the east, a juddering shadow rolled across the ground. It was two fields away but heading fast in their direction. Within seconds it had revealed itself as a wave of black and brown rats, racing madly towards them. The sisters stood, wary but not afraid, each grabbing something with which to defend themselves. Colette picked up her parasol and readied her finger on the catch. Any rat that came too close would be catapulted back where it had come from. Gertrude grabbed her bicycle pump and held it like a cricket bat, ready to knock each rat for six. Victoria stripped the twigs from a nearby branch. "Shoes, ladies," she said. They checked their laces were tight and tucked away, ready for action.

Rats swarmed through the picnic field, washing around the legs of screaming families. Fathers stood like lighthouses with their children hanging on to avoid getting washed away. Wives battled with their summer dresses. Suddenly the fresh breeze worked against them as their hems continued to billow, turning their legs into teasing snacks to tempt the hurrying horde of rats. Other than the sisters, only Jeb seemed equal to events, standing like a shield in front of the Misses Tinfeld and Cornigan, who each peeped over one of his massive shoulders as he held two toddlers over his head. The muscles in his arms rippled in the sun. Colette wished she had her camera with her before bringing her mind back to the job in hand. As it turned out, while the humans in the field were running in every direction, the rats moved in only one. They ignored the foods, the legs and the panic. Instead, they cut a line straight through the field, directly opposite from where they had entered. In about another minute, they would have vanished again. Then Mrs Delbing lost hold of her youngest, who sank to the ground near the sisters – right in the path of the oncoming flood of furry death. The young child clapped his hands in delight before stretching them out to pet the mess of dank fur. Victoria bounded forward. Rats squealed, and she felt several under her boots as she picked the child up and waded back to their eyrie on the knotted roots of Dame Holte's oak.

Then the rats were gone, leaving the panting crowd behind them. In just a few seconds they had all but disappeared through the hedge on the far side of the field, with an angry hissing of leaves.

"Not a bite taken," said Victoria. She referred to the food, rather than to her boots, which had been nibbled as she scooped up Delbing Junior. Self-defence, she thought. Looking around, she saw that the blankets and plates and detritus of the picnic were strewn throughout the field but hams, cakes and numerous knobbly chicken legs were plainly in evidence. It had been speculated that the hot weather was causing them to run out of food, leading them to attack out of desperation. But that was not the case here. The rats had not been hungry. They had been on a mission.

Gertrude had come to the same conclusion. "Quick," she said. As the crowd stirred back to life, the sisters were already off. They had parked their bikes right at the entrance to the field. Victoria was the last to mount, as she had to disentangle Delbing Junior and return him to his flushed mother. They pedalled furiously after the rats, following their quarry as close as the winding roads allowed. For now, the swarm was still in sight but quickly pulling ahead as the road sloped inland and uphill. The trail they left remained obvious and would do so until the bushes and grasses sprang back into shape. The sisters didn't stand a chance of keeping up. Luckily, they now knew where the swarm – the mischief – of rats was heading and they cycled as fast as they could to get there before the rats disappeared. They knew the destination, but not yet the purpose, and their analysis of the droppings and the field's pedology had not suggested any motive. They needed to discover what the rats did when they arrived.

"A straight line," mused Gertrude. It was one thing to see it on a map, quite another to see it in real life. The rats had not deviated an inch from their path and had soon left the sisters behind. Thankfully, they left all the livestock and crops behind too, scrabbling and swarming around anything in their way but otherwise ignoring it. The punctures in Victoria's boots testified that they would only react aggressively if attacked.

Victoria was glad of her reinforced toe caps, a precaution they had originally decided upon for work in the laboratory, where spilled chemicals reacted poorly with toes. They followed the trail of torn hedges and flattened crops towards Kelby's field. More striking than the flattened vegetation were the fields whose bovine inhabitants had stopped chewing the cud, grass falling out of their mouths, their lower jaws hanging open in shock.

"Really quite fantastic," said Victoria. "That's not how rats behave at all."

"I hope Jeb's okay," said Colette, which abruptly ended the conversation.

They were soon in that part of the countryside that belonged mostly to Kelby. Elsewhere the crops were already being harvested; here each field was still bursting with its bounty. Traditionally as the largest landowner – which is to say, the owner of the largest amount of land – his crop was gathered last. If the weather turned unexpectedly, he would better able to weather the loss of harvest than a smaller landowner, who might only have a field or two to support himself and his family. His fields were therefore still golden with wheat, through which the rats had flattened a causeway. He was in Turner's field when they dismounted from their bicycles. He carried a shotgun and a lit brazier.

Chapter 4

Rats' Patterns and Epigrapher's Missions

KELBY TURNED as he heard the sisters' bicycles skitter to a stop. He had enough presence of mind not to point the gun at them, but his shoulders were hunched and he looked defeated.

"What do they want?" he asked the ladies as they dismounted. "They came from over there." He pointed with a lit torch, its fire dim in the late July sun.

"Were you going to set them alight?" asked Victoria.

"Scare them away," said Kelby. "Burn them if they stayed. Look!" The three sisters looked where he pointed and could see the route the rats had taken, straight over the hill, past the town and into Kelby's field. Then they had disappeared. "They ran 'round and 'round and then they scattered."

The wheat had been trampled flat but was otherwise undamaged. The straight line of the rats' undeviating course towards Kelby's field had stopped as soon as they had reached it. They had turned it into a labyrinth of overlapping tracks which criss-crossed it from hedge to hedge. From where they stood, the sisters saw several paths branch off, as if the rats were following an invisible course, or compelled to create a particular pattern. Unfortunately, there was no way to see what the pattern might be, nor was there any indication of why the rats should suddenly be so urgently drawn to express themselves artistically. The sisters split up, each taking a different track to see as much as possible. They all ended up in the centre. They could tell it was the centre from the pressure of the ley line. Their metal toe caps amplified it and gave their toes pins-and-needles. Kelby's son Andrew had arrived at the field by then, also armed with a gun and a burning torch, with the same dazed look on his face that his father wore.

"We should cut it and take it in," said Andrew.

"No," said his father. "And nobody'll buy it anyway, because of the rats. It's as good as cursed."

Gertrude barked a quick laugh. "Grow up, man! Since when do rats perform witchcraft?" The two men were abashed by her use of the word, but couldn't think of anything to say.

"You know you have a ley line through this field?" asked Victoria. Kelby closed his eyes in resignation, as if that was the last straw. "No, that's a good thing," she said. "It means the rats are most likely being attracted to it, not to your crops. We just need to work out how."

And by whom? she thought, but did not say. Around them, the golden wheat was slowly rising from the ground. This was why no one had known where the rats were going. The trail disappeared quickly and there weren't many people other than Kelby and his labourers out here, none of whom wanted to gossip about rats at the expense of their harvest.

"It's springing back already," said Victoria. She spoke softly to get the Kelbys' attention. When she had it, she continued. "It's like this every time?"

"Exactly the same. We fluff it up a little more near the road before the reverend gets here. He doesn't like it. Says it's the Devil."

"He would!" said Gertrude.

"How did the reverend find out?" asked Colette.

"His friend saw it. Maybe hetold him."

"His friend?" asked Colette.

"Trousers," said Andrew without thinking. "I mean..."

"The professor?"

"Right."

So the curious de Glube already knew about this, drawn by his wanderings past the field at just the right time to see the rats converge. And the reverend knew once the professor told him. And neither of them had mentioned anything.

Colette unpacked her bag and started taking photographs. Long shots of the paths the rats had trampled as well as close-ups of the wheat. One of the most striking things was how neat the pathways were. Victoria measured the runs and Gertrude attempted to trace the path, drawing in her notebook as she walked, but the recovering crop obliterated it before she got very far. The rats had gone in circles, but there was more to it than that. They had created a pattern or performed some ritual movement, which ended over the ley line in the centre of the field. What did that mean? Well, it meant that the ley line was causing them to behave very strangely, but they had known that already. Animals, like humans, are more acutely aware of electromagnetic interference than they know. Therefore, a disturbance in the ley line's magnetic field could, in theory, cause the rats to behave oddly, but it wouldn't explain how it could call the rats to a specific location on a particular ley line from so far away, without other animals also being affected. Gertrude tapped her teeth with her pencil as she had a thought. Perhaps it was affecting other animals: the sudden infatuation of many of the town's housewives with young men that were physically adequate but otherwise unsuitable in every respect might be how it manifested itself in humans. Her eyes rested on Colette. But ley line or not, it was unusual for animals to create such neat patterns. She could check her star charts and solar readings to see if an increase in solar activity was somehow responsible, but she doubted it. She looked at the ground and couldn't help the feeling that the solution was staring her in the face. "Rats," she said.

They re-convened at home. Victoria had ridden back towards the picnic site to confirm her suspicions: the rats had not attacked anyone, and the bushes and crops along the way had sprung back into shape. The cows chewed the cud more thoughtfully than usual, but that was the only indication that something had happened.

"Food or panic would be most likely, except that they left everything at the picnic..." Victoria said as she joined Gertrude in the War Room.

"Or mating," said Gertrude, still following her own line of reasoning.

"... and they'd be more aggressive if they were panicking," said Victoria. The leather of her boots had been bitten through, but they did not display the frenzied tooth marks she would expect if the rats had been showing aggression towards each other. "We saw no dead rats in Kelby's field, nor anywhere else."

"Still," said Gertrude. "I wonder..." She knew she was close to the solution but couldn't put her finger on it. If only there was some way to discover the pattern. If Colette could be induced to wait in one of the trees at the edge of Kelby's field, then perhaps her silly camera would turn out to be useful after all. She suppressed a shudder at the thought. With Colette so smitten with the big lug from the feed shop, she might well swoon and break her neck, if he walked past.

"There's no obvious temporal schedule to the events that I can find," said Colette. "I visited some of Kelby's workers to ask what they had seen. Times of the day, days of the week. No correlation with weather or air pressure. No earth tremors or fires. Not even any fox-hunts to spook them, as the weather is too warm for the dogs. We don't have any sightings at night, but that's just as easily because no one has been up. Even assuming they did the same thing after nightfall, it wouldn't give us a pattern."

"No visible pattern," mused Victoria. "So, something invisible. Like the ley line."

"Unless there's something else in the field?" said Colette.

"Can we at least explain why the rats come from different directions? They came from the east today, while Mrs Sniffacre was up-ended at the top of town, which is a good two kilometres further north."

"The same story, I'm afraid," said Colette. "No pattern."

"But the sightings are all within a three-mile radius of Kelby's field, with a preponderance of sightings in the east, because that's where most people are. Kelby's people haven't been reporting on the rats for obvious reasons," said Victoria. "Most likely that's where the rats – or enough to create a critical mass – happen to be when it starts."

"A compulsion, then?" said Gertrude. Victoria and Colette agreed that that was currently the most accurate word. What precisely the compulsion was, remained a mystery. Which was satisfying as long as they could eventually resolve it. The sisters liked mysteries, which was why they had come to Hawkinge-By-Hythe in the first place. They hadn't seen many other places so filled with mysteries. The only irritation was the re-occurrence of the Dame Holte motif, but they didn't let it put them off. The locals could believe what they liked. They didn't have the training that the sisters did. And they would get to the bottom of the matter. Scientifically.

They toasted some cheese on bread, washed it down with masala chai, and retired to bed. The subconscious mind was a powerful tool, especially under the influence of cheese and ginger. With three of them pondering the matter, it could only be a matter of time before they worked it out. The rats didn't stand a chance.

People formed a queue outside the Alumière Apothecary the next morning. It quickly became clear that they were there to see the hero of the hour: Victoria, who had taken on the savage rat horde to save Delbing Junior. Everyone bought something, Gertrude made sure of that, but their customers were there to ask the Alumière sisters what they thought the town should do next. Victoria had always been the most popular of the three sisters at the apothecary as she had the best bedside manner, though now she was swamped and the other two were relegated to ringing up the till and wrapping up parcels of plasters and paracetamol, which props the locals bought as an excuse to hold court with Victoria.

"We should set her up with a crystal ball and charge a shilling a go," said Colette.

"Not everyone enjoys making an exhibition of themselves," sniffed Gertrude.

Then Mrs Delbing came in, bearing the other star of the previous day's drama. Mrs Delbing was the Town Gossip. This meant that she was not very popular, but that at the same time people were keen to stay on her good side. The sisters were less inclined to spare the busybody's feelings, and in return she made no secret of the fact that in her opinion only the devil himself could be behind three identical sisters. The assembled locals moved aside, not without some misgivings. This promised to be good, they only hoped that Victoria would be able to give as good as she got. She was, after all, the "nice" one.

For once, though, Delbing was being gracious. "Thank you, dear," she said to Victoria. "Junior would have been eaten alive if it weren't for you."

"Not at all," said Victoria, taken aback. "Glad to be of service."

"Really," said Mrs Delbing, hefting the apple of her eye in her arms. "He was this close to death." She held him out and swung him around to make sure everyone got a good look, forcing the crowd to duck or shy back.

"The rats really aren't dangerous," said Victoria. She had been explaining this all morning and was glad she had worn her other shoes – the ones that did not bear the teeth marks of the rats she had been required to step on – to work. "We followed them quite a distance, and they didn't harm anyone or anything."

"Disgusting creatures" said Delbing. "You'll do something about them, won't you?" Her eyes were furtive. She wasn't ready – just yet – to ask them to contact their infernal master to call off his minions. She hoped the Alumières would offer to do so of their own accord. But it was the very question that everyone wanted an answer to.

"I mean, you've got powders, haven't you?" Delbing nodded to the back of the store. "Something to get rid of them." What might have been mistaken for a sudden gust of wind blowing past the Apothecary, eager to escape before the trouble started, was more likely Gertrude inflating her lungs in the background as a necessary preliminary to delivering a fitting rebuke to the idea that the Alumières had set up shop to catch vermin.

"Let's see what the alderman has come up with first, shall we?" said Victoria quickly. Alderman Fawsick had convened another meeting for later that day. Apart from the publication of the reverend's letter the previous Friday, not much action had otherwise been undertaken so far.

Delbing cast a glance at Gertrude, nodded brusquely, and left.

The alderman had been one of their first visitors that morning. He had wanted to make sure that they would be attending the meeting. They were not council members, but he found it unthinkable to hold the meeting without them present. His discreet enquiries as to whether they had made progress were gently deflected. As yet, the sisters could add nothing further to the discussion other than that the rats were not dangerous if left alone. Which news the people of Hawkinge-By-Hythe did not wish to hear. Many of their customers had been at the picnic and were keen for "something against the Black Death," or an ointment against "weird plague bites," all of which had turned out to be scratches or bruises caused by clumsiness or panic, rather than the rats.

Still, Delbing Junior was as popular as his mother was unpopular, and none of those who had seen it could forget the sight of him sitting helplessly, the apparent focus of a horde of ferocious rats. The town went about its business with a sense of barely contained excitement all day, as they waited for the town hall event. It was like someone had vigorously shaken a bottle of carbonated water and hidden it back amongst its fellows in the crate. Someone was going to get a nasty surprise, but there was no way to tell who.

One of the few light spots was again provided by Professor de Glube (known to Andrew Kelby as "Trousers"). Unaware of recent events and oblivious to the mounting panic, he continued to stroll about the countryside, providing the townsfolk with a welcome distraction.

Of those in the Damme Billet, Old Smith was the first one to notice the professor that Monday, as he walked down the street outside the bar. "There goes Stained Glass Windows," he said as a blinding flash through the window lit up the dark wood of the counter and the motes of barley dust which hung suspended in the air around the assembled drinkers. Even the muffled tang of spilled beer briefly felt inspired to release a sharp tang of zesty orange, before the light vanished and it reverted to its usual fug of damp cellar. "And that's my boy," continued Smith. Outside a child's reedy voice attempted an interview of the professor with a view to determining if he rather dressed or painted himself each morning. The professor had passed.

The sisters were waiting for him. "Professor de Glube?" Gertrude was outside the Apothecary, watering its window boxes of lavender and sage as he approached. The commotion of the children who surrounded him quietened as they peeled away to interest themselves in a nearby dog. The dog had been on the chain since the rats had come to town and was grateful for company. The children, warned by their parents, kept their distance from the Alumières. They didn't mind the sisters at all and had no problem with the sisters' assertion that they were scientists. But the effect the Alumières had on their parents was undeniable, and not even the irascible reverend could hope for the respect they paid to the ladies. As far as the children were concerned, it was possible that scientists were even more dangerous than witches, which was fine by them. What was certain, however, was that Colette's recipe for itching powder was second to none and could, if she could be prevailed upon to make it available, easily end any dispute with the children from the next village over. Jeremy Tinfeld had been unlucky enough to experience it first-hand shortly after they arrived and still spoke about it in terms of reverent awe as a "three bath-er," referring to how much he had had to wash before he could bear to wear any clothes again.

"Professor?" Gertrude called a second time before he grew aware that he was being addressed. He appeared to be heading towards Bagnell's field – the scene of yesterday's picnic. Did that mean something? Gertrude meant to find out. The reverend remained a suspicious character in her mind and the professor was his friend.

"Good morning!" he called, but without any inclination to stop or even slow.

"A moment, if you please? You look a bit red, professor." *And blue and orange and...* Gertrude was not as conservative as the locals. She and her sisters had seen a lot more of the world. Even so, the pattern of his trousers was loud. They took the eye. Andrew Kelby had demonstrated a rare talent for anthroponomy on the previous day. This, indeed, was Trousers. Gertrude handed the man some sun lotion. He beamed at her and smeared it liberally over his face.

"Thank you." He handed it back.

"We haven't met yet. How do you enjoy our town?"

"It's beautiful," he said. "And so... important."

Gertrude and her sisters had their own reasons for finding Hawkinge-by-Hythe interesting, but she hadn't expected others to make the same connection.

"You're certainly seeing plenty of it. I've seen you out and about every day. In this weather!"

"It's not a problem. I am on a mission!"

"Really?"

"Oh, yes." He stopped, and Gertrude thought he would clam up, but he was looking towards Main Street. His brow furrowed. "Poor woman!"

Gertrude looked to see who had caught his eye. Mrs Sniffacre was coming into view now. She had recovered well from her shock and was even smiling to herself. The professor leaned in conspiratorially. His face was white from the sun lotion and Gertrude momentarily had the disconcerting impression that a football was trying to kiss her. "She has seen them, you know. The rats."

"*Has* she?"

"She has." He nodded decisively, lifting and dropping his chin twice, most eloquently. He looked around and lowered his voice. "I too have seen them."

"*Have* you?"

"But *shhh!* It upsets the reverend. He thinks of the Devil."

"And you don't?"

"Pssssh! Little rats! But the farmer was upset too. So, I have said nothing to anybody. Are you well, Madam?" This last was addressed to the approaching Mrs Sniffacre, who startled slightly before offering them both a wave. "And now I must be off, on my mission."

"Must you?"

"Epigraphy, Madam!"

"Oh, how interesting! I'd love to hear more about it. We get so few interesting men around here. Wouldn't you agree, Mrs Sniffacre? And I was about to make some tea, anyway."

"Actually, I need to –"

"Mrs Sniffacre! Please, won't you ask the professor to be a dear and join us?" Gertrude already had the professor by the arm and Colette was suddenly holding Mrs Sniffacre's laden basket.

"Ah, there are two of you!" said the professor.

"Three," said Victoria, as the group entered the shop.

"Three? Oh, now I understand what the reverend was talking about, but you mustn't be angry with him. He sees his little Devils everywhere, poor man."

He twisted out of Gertrude's surprised grip to offer a bow to Mrs Sniffacre. "De Glube, Madam!" His face was still greasy with sun lotion.

"If you say so," said Mrs Sniffacre. "I mean: Mrs Sniffacre. Well, Sniffacre. Jennet."

"It's not the first time I've seen them, you know," said the professor, speaking to them both.

"*Really?*" said Gertrude as she ushered him to a seat in the small kitchen behind the shop. Victoria closed the door and Colette grinned. The professor was about to be stripped of his secrets.

Chapter 5

Whistle When You Say That At The Town Hall

THE TOWN HALL EVENT didn't disappoint. Only Mr Carde later had any regrets, having missed an opportunity to cash in on his supply of rock sulphur. As he explained before the judge afterwards, while giving his testimony on the ensuing riot, matters could never have come to such a head under the influence of beneficial rock sulphur, which could be relied upon to tame the wildest disposition, as well as protecting against skin irritations in puppies. His testimony concluded with an exhortation to the alderman to lay in a supply against future flare-ups. That way he could flatter himself that he had done his utmost in the way of future proofing further events against potential free-for-alls. The Constable, acting as bailiff, was clearly interested, but the alderman demurred. He doubted that the people of Hawkinge-By-Hythe would agree to drink a bowl of dog water before entering Town Hall. It was tempting, of course. But no.

The sisters were among the last to arrive on the evening of the town hall event. The crowd was jittery and displayed a tendency to cast nervous glances at the floor. Occasional shrieks punctuated the murmur, as children or furniture brushed against unsuspecting legs. The rats had left their mark on Hawking-by-Hythe.

Alderman Fawsick sat on the raised dais at the front of the hall. He looked well. He had taken to the sport of bicycling after his unwilling introduction to it (facilitated by the sisters, who had required his vehicle for other purposes), and it gave his cheeks a red glow, which was an improvement over their previous milky custard sheen. Colette liked the effect it had on his hair, which stood whisked back from his face, giving it the appearance of a stubborn dandelion clock, the seeds of which refused to leave the parent head. A kind of friendship had sprung up between the sisters and the alderman, who, though he was the most important person in town, did not have many close friends. For his part, he was grateful that their help had helped him resolve several tricky issues, where nobody else seemed to know what to do – other than Reverend Gresstart, whose cures tended to be worse than the disease.

Fawsick was flustered. The town's panic was boiling over into anger. They had been "attacked" right at Dame Holte's burial site. It was only a matter of time before pitchforks were dusted off. His best chance had been that the sisters would find a way, but he had spoken to them before the meeting started and had his hopes dashed on that account. Victoria's research had uncovered a similar incident in Germany. Though the sources were unreliable, the matter had been chalked up to the work of a gifted if immoral animal trainer. None of them believed that that was what was happening in the current case. There was something else behind it. Something unusual. Something weird. Just the kind of thing they were most interested in, as a matter of fact.

There was little help to be had from the other members of the council either. Their primary qualification for the job was an air of detachment, which shielded them from responsibility. With the exception of the Muirs, who had somehow remained council members despite not having been physically present in Hawkinge-By-Hythe for at least the last ten years, they were all assembled around Fawsick on the dais. The Reverend Gresstart insisted on sitting alone on Fawsick's right. Mr Cornigan sat to his left. (Mrs Cornigan, who had insisted they arrive extra early, enjoyed pride of place next to Jeb in the audience.) Then there was Mrs Jumpage. Then Mr Oaten. The only item on the credit side of the ledger, as far as Fawsick was concerned, was that the reverend was distracted by the crowd's attention to his visitor. Even the small but vocal group, which served as his biggest fans, were eyeing the professor askance.

Professor de Glube sat near the front of the otherwise crowded hall within a small but invisible bubble. The people closest to him did their best to move away even as more people piled in. He seemed unaware of anything wrong and made use of the conspicuously empty chair beside him for his notebook. Gertrude kept her eye on him. At one point he looked around and gave them a wave, but seemed disappointed not to find whatever it was he was searching for. Colette waved back, but the Alumières remained sensibly at the rear of the hall where they were better able to observe. De Glube had shown Gertrude his notebook as he had talked to her and Mrs Sniffacre. As well as various etchings and notes regarding some of the epithets he had been collecting – and it did not escape her notice that he was secretive about several others – it contained a list of phrases, useful for a man in a foreign country as well as several later entries that a man in a foreign country had clearly been given by people with a childish if effective sense of humour. If he used those here, there was a good chance things would come to blows. For their part, the sisters had unanimously decided that if they were called upon to make a contribution, it would be Victoria's role to act as spokesperson. Gertrude was impatient with the obstinacy of the many-headed, when it was determined to make a fool of itself, and Colette had allowed herself to be roped in to act as official photographer for the event. In fact, she had insisted upon it. Her only regret was that she did not have colour plates with which to capture the glory of the professor's trousers. The town hall was one of Hawking-by-Hythe's more stately buildings, whereby stately meant packing in as much dark wood as possible. The professor's trousers shone. "If we could put trousers like those on the rats," said Colette. "Then we shouldn't have to worry about losing them."

Contrary to protocol, the proceedings were opened by Mrs Delbing. Before the constable could stand up to demand silence, which is how they usually did things, she had lifted Little Delbing above her head and requested the assembled company to marvel at his continued survival. She continued to talk, the gist of which was to imply that the child was clearly blessed with an overabundance of natural talent, quick wits and force of character, unusual in one so young. She did not address the point that most interested the crowd: where the child might have received these blessings, assuming, as they did not, that the theory of genetic inheritance answered that question adequately. Nor did she now mention that it was Victoria who had pulled the child out of the way of the oncoming rats.

"But what are we going to do?" she wailed. "Other children might not be so lucky."

"The constable here," said the alderman. "Has been working tirelessly on this case."

The constable jerked upright in his chair. He had only just settled back with his arms folded and his ankles crossed over each other. The audience jeered. They rightly felt that this sort of task was not for the police, certainly not in the shape of the constable, who was a fine chap but whose talents lay more in the direction of driving slowly after a cycling alderman, in case he should tire, or announcing "the meeting may begin," than in stemming natural disasters and plagues, into one of which category the advent of the rats must surely fall.

"Well, who else has a suggestion?" asked the alderman. He unwillingly looked towards the reverend, who could normally be relied upon to have an opinion. But Professor de Glube was apparently jotting down some of the more ribald comments he could hear, and the crowd was paying him far too much attention for Gresstart's liking. The reverend harrumphed and scowled at anyone who caught his eye.

"Action!" said Mrs Delbing. "Action is what we need!"

There were cheers from the audience. The memory of the flashing bodies and pink noses put the crowd on her side.

"But what do you suggest?" asked the alderman.

"My granny –"

The crowd cut her off with an involuntary collective groan.

"My granny," she started again, "said that sudden rats is war. There was rats before the Vikings and there was rats before the French."

"Tell Granny to put her musket down, there's no wars coming!" said someone. The resulting laughter would have daunted anyone else.

"And there have been outside influences in the area recently." Delbing was looking at Professor de Glube as she said this, but everyone knew that she was thinking about the Alumière sisters too. The snap of Gertrude's teeth as Delbing paused, acted as a warning slap for the crowd. "They could be spies... Could be, is all I'm saying." But the crowd had abandoned her. This was the Delbing they all knew.

"Never mind that. How do we get rid of them?" Fawsick capitalised on the crowd's silence.

"My granny said to write a note!" said Delbing.

"The reverend has already contacted The Times..." said Fawsick.

"No! Write the rats a note. Ask them to leave."

"My Gran said to always whistle when you said 'rat'," said someone in the crowd.

"My Granddad said to ask to borrow money! That clears them out pretty sharpish!"

"Get Old Smith to tell the rats one of his jokes!"

"You're being silly! You write a note to the rats and ask them to move somewhere else. Put it on their rat hole and once they bring it to their rat king, the rats leave." Mrs Delbing was used to laughter, but the whistling of the crowd whenever she said 'rat', effectively stopped her from saying more.

Colette took several wonderful shots of whistling villagers, their lips pursed and their eyes crinkled closed in mirth. Then the reverend stood, and they quietened. The town hall was packed, and the room was suddenly very warm and stuffy, as they tried to get their breath back.

"I do not have time for this," he said. He cast a meaning glance at the alderman. He inflated his lungs, by which means he clearly signalled that friends of correct capitalisation should cover their ears. The Reverend Gresstart felt *Moved*. "This Town," he said, "is being Visited by a Plague!" Gresstart was an impressive figure, with his long thin nose, dark eyes and hair which looked longer than it was. He appeared almost Byronic. A rather grumpy and party-pooping Byron, but still... Furthermore, what he said perfectly captured the general feeling of the meeting. And he had managed to take their attention away from Professor de Glube, though the man *insisted* on continuing to make notes.

"This Town," he said, "Is Lax."

The reverend's regulars, which skewed generally older and/or more respectable, murmured agreement. Other members of the town (generally those who skewed younger and/or who felt that a touch of laxity needn't automatically be considered a bad thing should they ever spot some), looked less convinced. Nonetheless, in the absence of further suggestions, they were willing to take his word for it. Colette joined her sisters at the back of the hall.

Relations between the reverend and the sisters had been tense from the start. They had nothing against religion in moderation, but found the man himself untrustworthy. He was certainly up to something. "Even if he's just using his holy water to brush his teeth," as Colette had put it. For his part, he considered them a nuisance and the worst type of modern women, interested only in tearing down traditions and lacking in respect for their betters.

"These Rats are Here to Tell us Something," said the reverend. Now that the crowd had got its fit of anger and bout of the sillies out of the way, they were willing to listen to him, even though they had received their weekly dose just the day before. His eyes strafed the crowd, though he kept them on the front rows, well away from the Alumière sisters. He knew when to pick his battles. "We must Root Out the Evil," he said. "We must Return to Traditional Values, to the Word of the Good Lord!" The mood shifted again. The crowd had expected more than the usual advertisement for the reverend's own business. He was losing them, but something had touched a chord. Perhaps it was the combination of the words 'root' and 'evil'. The sisters couldn't pinpoint where it started, but two words passed through the hall, growing in volume as they rippled back and forth, echoing off the walls. The words were "Dame Holte". The reverend let it gather. It was adjacent to what he had been trying to say, but undeniably apposite. An illustration of the lesson he wished them to learn. He decided to use it to drive home his point. "Holte's Revenge! She's Sending the Rats. We must Stick Together," he said, but already another word was coursing through the room.

The word was "Witches!" The townsfolk knew better than to suggest that the Alumière sisters themselves were witches (though in the privacy of their own minds, they preferred to leave their options on the matter open). Unfortunately, a few people were unable to prevent themselves from eyeing their black-clad figures.

"Now listen." The alderman stood, raising his hands, imploring for calm to prevail.

"Witches!" murmured the crowd.

"Right," said Gertrude. Gresstart wasn't the only one who could give a speech. And although they had walked to the Town Hall, she had her metal bicycle pump in her hand again. Victoria was briefly tempted to let events take their course, but followed her sister to the front of the hall. Somebody would have to stop the crowd from getting hurt. Mrs Delbing had asked that morning if Victoria didn't have any powders, and she certainly did. Any funny business and the crowd would get two full pockets' worth. Colette's camera continued to click, but now she held a sturdy metal tripod under her arm as she took a final image, preserving the frozen instant where Gertrude prepared to tell the crowd exactly what she thought of them.

A scream averted the immediate disaster. Mrs Delbing had backed away from the advancing Alumière sisters and now pointed to the professor, who looked up from his notebook in surprise. "He drew a spell," said Delbing. The crowd, already sceptical of the professor's *bona fides,* now turned on him. He was too bemused to protect himself, and someone had ripped his notebook out of his hand before he even knew what was happening. From their new position at the base of the dais the sisters saw the professor's illuminated bloomers become the centre of a group of hooligans, led by Delbing, who had once again left Junior to fend for himself. Mrs Sniffacre, who had just arrived, screamed, and the sisters rolled up their sleeves, preparatory to wading in. The reverend was even more upset. He demanded respect and didn't enjoy having his reputation impugned, even by proxy. As the sisters battled their way from the left through the hands grabbing De Glube, he made full use of his size and holy clothes to more or less bodily rescue his friend, carrying the flaccid professor onto the podium.

"We Must Root Out The Evil," he roared, falling into full capitalisation as the only way to express his feelings. "Root It Out." In the continuing melee below, hands grabbed at the sisters, even as the professor's notebook flapped onto the dais, winking its dog-ears at its owner. But steel-capped boots are a wonderful thing, and matters quickly settled. The reverend held out the book, ignoring the look of anguish on his friend's face as he paged through it. There was no sign of a spell in there and even Mrs Delbing was temporarily abashed at the look the reverend gave her. He had entered full Pulpit Mode. End Days. Enemies Among Us. Disciples of Deceit. There was No Other Explanation for a Friend of the Church being singled out as the Object of Suspicion. All the fault of Satan's Insidious Minions: the Rats, which needed to be Rooted Out.

Eventually he calmed enough to return to standard English capitalisation, and a muted discussion of how to practically tackle the matter of the rats was enjoined. To an onlooker it would seem civil, perhaps even boring, but the Alumière sisters could feel eyes on them all the time. The Dunsloes, Mrs Sniffacre and a few others came to stand by them. Jeb joined Colette, which only got Gertrude worked up again. But the damage had been done.

Then Mr Oaten mentioned a friend of his who owned kennels and "absolute scads" of dogs. Victoria sighed and reminded the townsfolk that the rats were unpleasant but peaceful as long as they were not interfered with. Her objections were overruled by the mob. Their blood was up and it was useless to explain that the rats had not attacked anyone. The council decided unanimously that as many dogs as possible would be brought in to sniff out and eradicate the rats, and as the crowd had not yet completely given up their original suspicions, the alderman weakly promised that something would be done "about Dame Holte" (he did not say "the witch"), if matters persisted thereafter.

So far, the town hall meeting had been no worse than the sisters had been expecting. Rather below than above average in terms of excitement, in fact. And it was extremely unlikely that the dogs would even get a sniff of the rats, so matters were drawing to a satisfactory close, when Professor de Glube decided it was time to thank the people of Hawkinge-By-Hythe for the warm welcome they had extended to him. The eagerness of the locals to help him with the intricacies of their unusually idiosyncratic language; the intense interest of the children in the customs and clothes of his own country and, regardless of where he went, the smiles of pure joy on everyone's face when they saw him coming, had touched him deeply. He made copious use of the friendly colloquialisms which the people of Hawkinge-By-Hythe had taught him, and even ad-libbed a few of the newer phrases that he had picked up in the recent discussions and rough-housing.

It was plain that he meant every word – and *that's* what started the riot.

Chapter 6

The Phoenix Rises...

THE DOGS WERE A BUST from the start. Almost forty came, the pick of the bunch according to Mr Oaten, but they found nothing. They ran up against the same problem as the Alumière sisters: there was no schedule or pattern to the rats' appearances, and therefore nothing for them to do other than wait. But the scent of the rats was still strong and drove the dogs into a frenzy. They wee'd on everything and snapped at anyone other than their handlers, who found themselves dragged through Kelby's crops, and after two days he put his foot down – no more dogs on his property. And that was that. It was the best possible outcome. He agreed with the Alumières that further antagonising the rats, which were already functioning under some sort of intense compulsion, was not the best way to deal with things.

Over the course of the following week, Gertrude, Victoria and Colette had been out several times to visit Kelby's field, but also without success. As the labourers started to harvest the crops, there was a feeling that time was running out. Why this should be a bad thing was not clear, but the sisters felt that it was important to intervene before the rats had completed whatever task it was that had been assigned to them. On Colette's request, Kelby had fixed a ladder to a tree at the edge of Turner's field. Jeb joined her in the evenings sometimes, for photography lessons. They learned from Andrew Kelby that the town's womenfolk passed by more often than usual, or at least more than he would have expected, now that he was on the alert for anything unusual. Gertrude put this down to Jeb's presence. On the occasion of one of the photography lessons, Jeb was startled by the sudden appearance of De Glube and his young followers and was glad of the protection of the wheat, as he was not properly dressed to receive visitors. The professor passed on with a cheery wave, however. When Colette later questioned her troupe of investigators, they told her that he was en route to a local lychgate, out near Bleddsham, rumoured to feature an inscription by philosopher and alchemist, John Dee himself. She was more interested that he had made a number of other stops and measurements on the way. When he was making his notes was the only time he lost his geniality, insisting the children stay back while he did so.

Victoria meanwhile had turned the focus of her researches from de Glube to Gresstart and his ancestors. Whatever the professor was up to, it was unlikely to involve the rats, while the reverend, despite his public denunciations, seemed not to have mentioned the fact that he knew exactly where they could be found to anyone. The man was up to something.

And Jeb was becoming suspicious of Mrs Sniffacre. The old dear wasn't herself at all anymore, though she continued to call around to buy animal feed. She looked as if she wanted to tell him something. Did she want to confess to feeding the rats? Colette agreed to look into the matter for him.

The rats kept a low profile all week, and people started to breathe easy again. The following weekend was the Summer Bank Holiday, and the forecast indicated a break in the weather just afterwards. Perhaps they had made it safely through the summer after all.

The Summer Bank Holiday was the highlight of the year and everyone attended the celebrations in Bagnell's field. After the first few cups of tea or beer, they even started to enjoy themselves, despite the threat of sudden rats. Well, almost everyone. Chloe Dunsloe had offered to babysit the Alumière's two-headed calf, Curly, as the animal was even more outspoken than Gertrude, and had been forbidden from attending the celebrations. The sisters feared, with some justification, that Curly wouldn't be able to keep his mouths shut and his standing with the alderman was already quite shaky. "Well, whose fault is that?" he asked, as he had been firmly against the use of the alderman in a recent case of "possession," but he was overruled and the matter was closed.

A large tent housed the day's entertainments. Two smaller tents provided refreshments. One served tea and the other served festival-strength beer. At a little under three percent alcohol, it had the opposite effect to that intended, as everyone felt it tasted a little watery, and they drank more to make up for this deficit.

The main attraction this year was the Phoenix, which excited gasps from everyone, even before they arrived, as it could be seen from miles away. It was a hot-air balloon with an enormous gaily-coloured bag. It wafted over the field and merrymakers, pulling at its tethering. It was offering rides and later there was to be a show as one of the operators was a stunt parachutist.

The Phoenix's bag was maroon and navy and gold, with orange trim at the bottom and the top. By the time the sisters arrived, the children had mostly decided how they would each update their repertoire to include references to the balloon while discussing haberdashery with their guest from Luxembourg. A man in a cap and shirt sleeves stood in the basket, while a lady in a white blouse, leather waistcoat and trousers waited on the ground. She wore a scarf knotted about her neck for a piratical air, which suited her perfectly. She was busy protecting the stout stake driven into the ground, which prevented the balloon from drifting away. All that was missing was the rocking of waves and a sword flashing in her hand.

The ascents were popular and apart from an awkward moment at the beginning – Alderman Fawsick had positioned himself at the start of the queue to open the ride but the operators had automatically assumed that he intended to be the first one in, and were wondering how best to dissuade him – things passed off without a hitch. From the air the countryside was visible to the coast, and all the way across the channel the mists enshrouding Nord-Pas-de-Calais gave France a mysterious air.

Colette wasn't interested in the views, but the balloon struck her as being just what they needed to sort out the rat problem, assuming they made an appearance – and she had a feeling they would. Only Kelby's field was left to harvest, which meant that the rats did not have much time left to practise their pattern-making. She joined the queue, while Gertrude and Victoria talked with De Glube and Mrs Sniffacre, who appeared skittish. The balloon operators took it in turns to go up with their customers, and Colette paid the lady her shilling as she entered the basket with her.

The townsfolk had been diligently assuaging their thirst with the healthy, practically alcohol-free beer. It must have been the healthy nutrients it contained, which caused them all to find life hilarious. Not a single passenger had ascended thus far without being accompanied by a hearty stream of encouragement along the lines of "Up she goes!" "Send us a postcard, won't you?" and "Wa-heeeeeeeeyyy!" There were also recurring renditions of "Nearer My God To Thee," though this sounded like it was being produced on a gramophone nearing the end of its useful lifetime. It slowed, sped up, and stopped and started at compositionally interesting spots. Colette was spared all of this. One of the men called "Good luck, Ma'am!" and up she went.

It was like flying. She concentrated on the feeling for a full minute. Gravity was present, and logically the air surrounding the balloon could not be much different to that at ground level, but the feeling of freedom was inexpressible. The wind blew colder and fresher on her face, and watching the ground detach itself from her feet was among the most novel experiences she had ever had. The sight of her two sisters dwindling away below her caused a momentary pang.

"Lovely, isn't it?" said Kaye, the lady balloonist.

Colette nodded. "May I?" she asked, indicating the camera.

Kaye nodded. "Be quick though, if you can. Jerry'll get thick if he finds out he missed a chance to be photographed." Kaye stood up straighter, wrapped an arm through one of the supports and smiled. A buffet of wind ruined the photograph.

"Almost," said Colette. The camera was a bit sensitive. Colette peered through the viewfinder to try again. Over the balloonist's shoulder was a shadow. She looked up, then back. Below them in the distance the rats were swarming. She snapped the photo.

"Look!" She pointed.

"What on Earth is that?"

"Rats," said Colette.

"Nice day for it," said Kaye. "Poor old Jerry, on the ground. He's terrified of them!"

"Can we follow them? It's rather serious."

"The balloon's moored to that peg."

"Imagine how thick Jerry would get, if he found out he missed a chance to be photographed heroically saving the day."

Kaye smiled. "Ready, then?" She had a sword, or at least a machete. She posed for a moment. The camera clicked. She leaned out dangerously and slashed at the line. Colette took another photograph, and the balloon soared higher. "See you at home," shouted Colette to her sisters. They stared at her. Victoria in surprise, Gertrude with a look that said that this was really too much. Jeb was there too. His usually handsome figure suffered terribly from the foreshortening effect of looking at him from above. His broad shoulders tapered away, almost to doll's feet. She snapped a quick picture of him for posterity and then got down to business. "You too, Jerry," shouted Kaye. "If you're lucky!"

The sensation of movement was somewhat similar to standing in a boat, but there the fundament was water and thus unreliable. Here they stood in a basket and between them and the ground: nothing.

Colette didn't have time to enjoy it though. The breeze pulled them closer to the rats. She documented the rats' progress, happy that they were coming from further south this time and therefore unlikely to pass through Bagnell's field. She wouldn't miss any excitement. She leaned on the edge of the basket beside Kaye. They would have to be male rats. Their narrow brush with them at the picnic confirmed that these were Norwegian rats, and it was at least conceivable that the more placid males were, somehow, being controlled to act in this fashion. It would be even more difficult to induce the more curious females to behave so out of character. She saved the rest of her film for when they reached their destination.

It was Kelby's field, of course. The rats reached it first, continuing to run as they poured inside. The entire field was overrun with hundreds and hundreds of pulsing driven rats. Once they were all in, they circled the boundaries of the field, flattening the crop in a perfect circle. Then another one, slightly smaller, then the animals broke apart into streams, dividing to create more circles, lines. A spell. Kaye backed away from what she saw. Colette took pictures. This was worse than they had feared.

Chapter 7

And Makes An Heroic Emergency Landing

"CAN YOU STEADY IT?" Colette asked. The balloon was being buffeted again and she wanted to distract Kaye, so she wouldn't see the pattern too clearly. There was something very wrong happening in the field, and it wasn't the sort of thing a healthy young girl should have to see.

The balloon continued to lose altitude, threatening to land right where the mischief of rats was thickest. On top of everything else, the balloon had crested the hill on which Kelby's field was situated and a cold northern wind pushed it down. Kaye was busy with ropes and ballast, lightening the load and steering the balloon as best she could while it dropped. She gave the rats only the briefest glance. "There is no way we are landing down there," she said.

"Certainly not." Colette took another photo. By now they were directly over the rat infestation, though only a few metres higher than if she had been waiting in the tree Kelby had prepared for her. She forced herself to let go of the basket and took a picture of Kaye manning the ropes. Then the rats finished their work and fled. One moment they were spinning around creating a meticulous design in Kelby's crops and the next they scattered in every direction, like an extremely fragile black porcelain bowl smashing onto a tiled floor, its shards racing in every direction. They had been released. Colette took a final photograph.

From up here it was unmistakable. The rats had run arrow straight to Kelby's field. Or rather, to the ley line which ran through it. The design was far too intricate to be perceived from ground level, but its essence was the double outer circles containing writing and a central figure, wide hipped and tangle-haired. She turned her back on the picture of a woman as large as a field. "Can you take us back?"

"No," said Kaye. "But I can take us over there, away from the rats. Do you have anything left to record an heroic emergency landing?"

Colette might sport the topmost button on her blouse in an occasionally unconventional manner, but she was an Alumière and always came prepared. "Aye, aye, Captain," she said. "Wait till Jerry sees these!"

It took another three hours before she got back to the house. First there was the emergency landing, which had been thrilling. Kaye had steered them to a field further down the hill. The trees had rushed towards them from below, then, as they dropped lower, they had whistled past on either side, before the ground jumped up in slow motion towards them like an eager dog through treacle. Colette took pictures of it all. She stowed her camera and held on tightly as Kaye manipulated the balloon. Grass whipped their basket and then they were back on the ground. Her body complained that the gravity was suddenly very strong.

After that, it had been necessary to take more photographs of the emergency landing. One thing Colette had quickly discovered was that although the camera could not lie, it didn't always accurately record the mood of events. So, with Kaye's help they re-staged some of the photos from the ground, including one where Kaye had prepared to jump out of the basket shortly before touchdown, her knife between her teeth.

After that they said their goodbyes, Colette promising to forward on the photos once they had been developed. Jerry was sure to be already on his way, and Kaye hated leaving the balloon unattended.

When Colette arrived at home, her skirt and blouse were rather dishevelled and she was breathing heavily after her trek. "Well?" said Victoria, as she fed Curly a chocolate eclair through the window of the War Room. The ladies bought them for Chloe, who claimed to love them but was never able to eat much.

Curly had had a grand time since the Alumières had left. Chloe had told him all about the polychromatic professor and even prepared a portfolio of tailoring sketches to show what Curly would look like if he were to follow the professor's example. She may have exaggerated the trousers somewhat, or else it was her sense of fairness that required her to use every pencil in her colouring box, but Curly had fallen in love with the glorious plus-fours she had conjured. He intended to broach the matter as soon as possible, but had waited for Colette as he felt sure she could be relied upon to plead his case.

Gertrude continued to write one of her Society letters and ignored her sister, who, she could tell from here, was inadequately buttoned.

"Witchcraft!" said Colette.

"Uh-oh!" said Curly with one mouth. His other mouth licked the last of the eclair's cream off the plate and he disappeared.

Chapter 8

A Handsome Soldier And The Worst Kind Of Evil

"THE RATS RETURNED to Kelby's field. Same as last time. They ran around and around, then disappeared. They were creating a symbol in the wheat by trampling it flat. Once it was done, they scattered, almost burst apart. Once whoever was controlling them let them go." Gertrude sniffed. Colette had sat down and was sketching what she had seen. "I have photos as well, of course, but this is what I saw. A sigil. It takes up the whole field, which is why we couldn't see it from the ground. From the air, it's obvious. Someone wants to bring the dead back to life."

Gertrude needed to say something or burst, she hated unscientific talk. Colette took pity on her. "I know I probably shouldn't have gone off like that, but I saw the swarm from the balloon. They were too far away, thank Goodness, for us to have caught up with them by bicycle and I thought this was the best way to find out what they are doing." Gertrude was mollified but not yet ready to unbend. She sniffed again. Colette saw red. "And you wouldn't have been much use, with that allergy!" she said. She had finished drawing and stormed out of the room.

Two circles. One inside the other. Thick writing filled the space between them, but it was not the demon's name. They were runes. It was an incantation. The sigil was in the inner circle, an unholy combination of conjoined circles, straight and barbed lines, channelling the force of belief. "Saleos," said Victoria, handing the image to Gertrude. "Hell's handsome soldier. And a Rune of Re-awakening. It *is* witchcraft, I'm afraid. Someone here believes in the worst type of evil."

Gertrude gave it a glance. "They can believe what they like," she said. "But re-vivification is not something people should do, willy-nilly. There are all sorts of considerations. Practical. Legal." She sniffed. "Moral, too, I suppose." She raised her voice. "But there are always people who think they can just go off and do whatever they want, regardless of anyone else!" She dismissed the topic with another sniff.

"Perhaps it's a summer cold," said Victoria. She took the teapot from the stove. "Can I tempt you with a hot drop?"

"Harrumph!" said Gertrude. "Yes. Please."

Now that Colette had provided them with the exact purpose of the rat's behaviour, the sisters were confident of quickly solving the matter. They had the motive. Working backwards from that should soon provide them with the 'who'. Victoria buried herself in her books, digging further into the town's history while the townsfolk were surprised by how chatty

Gertrude had become, displaying a disarming interest in their families and heritage. Mrs Sniffacre, who had lived alone since her husband died, particularly enjoyed the attention when she came into town. It was Victoria who provided the next piece of the puzzle on the evening of the third day. Colette was making the most of the daylight and took off after tea each evening, and Victoria had to wait for her to return before she could tell them what she had found. When she did return, the second button was also undone and her cheeks once again flushed. She didn't say where she had been but put her camera on the table and relayed greetings from Jeb. Gertrude caught Victoria's eye and refrained, for now, from commenting.

Victoria had been piecing together snippets of information gleaned from official records and newspaper reports. "The further back one goes," she said, "the less fussy they were with regard to what they published." Victoria had gone back some 400 years.

"Dame Holte is not, of course, buried under the Hanging Oak in Bagnell's farm. She was buried on quite the other side of town. Back then the land used to belong to a family called Turner, as Kelby said. A poor family. They were related to the Holtes by marriage. And the Holtes had been doing very well for themselves for a long time. Once the witchcraft trial started, the Holte family mostly left the area, but the Turners stayed. It looks like the Turners agreed to bury Dame Holte's body on their land for want of a better place. She won't have been eligible for a spot in the graveyard, and she had been a Turner herself, originally. And the Holtes had money to spare, to pay for the Turners to take care of things." Victoria paused. "But it didn't seem to do them any good. Things went from bad to worse for the family. Perhaps people found out what they had done, or else they felt it was now safe to take out their feelings on the Turners, once the Holtes had left. Eventually the Turners lost the small plot of land that they had and their name faded from the history books."

"It's just like Kelby to name his field after the family he bought it from, even if they haven't been around for 400 years." Gertrude approved of this academic tendency.

"And is outliving some men really all Dame Holte did?" asked Colette.

Victoria shrugged. "Well, it was at least a dozen men. Nothing definitively 'occult,' mind you, but she was undoubtedly bad for male life expectancy in the area." Gertrude looked at the map they had hung on the wall, putting it all together. "And here's an interesting fact, which probably isn't relevant at the moment," said Victoria. "The only member of the Holte family who stayed in Hawkinge-By-Hythe, was the Dame's sister, who had married a Gresstart and made herself respectable."

"And the legend of her being under the Oak Tree in Bagnell's field?" said Colette.

"Just that. A legend. She was hung there, but not buried. A few sightings were reported, and over time people forgot the actual location. Why not under the scary oak tree?"

Gertrude rose and stalked to the map. She placed her finger on a ley line and traced its progress across the paper as Victoria continued. "Where Dame Holte is actually buried," she said, even as Gertrude's finger stopped moving in the centre of a wheat field, " is in the field that used to belong to the Turner family, since bought by the Kelby family. Dame Holte was Turner's daughter before she married – for the last time – Mr Holte. She was buried on her own land. Which had a ley line running through it. Which was where the rats have been creating their cereal sigil. The Rune of Re-Awakening!"

Dame Holte had been executed on the tree in Bagnell's field shortly after the Summer Bank Holiday 400 years ago, after her latest husband had suffered a heart attack. According to his relatives, the heart attack had been caused by the sight of his new bride kissing a dog the size of a bull, which smelled of sulphur and had the face of an angry old man on its back end. It was the last straw. The Holte family had sponsored the annual Summer Bank Holiday entertainments for as long as anyone could remember, and his wife was sentenced without even the pretence of it being a fair trial. Everyone knew that she was a witch, after all.

Though sceptical of the supernatural undertone of events, it seemed likely that anyone who believed enough in demons and witchcraft to attempt to bring a dead person back to life would inevitably see the 400th anniversary as auspicious for their purposes. Kelby revealed that the crop was due to be harvested the day after, which confirmed it. So, the sisters now had the 'why', and the 'where' and the 'when.' Who and how were still under debate. They were staunch supporters of the scientific method and hoped to resolve the 'how' by direct observation. Until then Gertrude fumed to herself about 'black magic.' It was a ridiculous conceit. Knowledge was neither inherently good nor evil, it was the purpose for which it was used that gave it its moral character. And magic was just a word admitting defeat, that one had given up on trying to determine the explanation. But the sisters knew all about the 'rules' of magic, and whoever was controlling the rats would require a sacrifice.

And that bit, after all, did have some scientific basis. Nothing to do with magic. It was physics, pure and simple:

the law of the conservation of energy, as formulated by du Châtelet. Energy could neither be destroyed nor created, merely transferred between forms. If Hawkinge-By-Hythe's modern-day pied piper hoped to transform the body of a dead witch into that of a living witch, it would need a source of energy which would be transferred from the living sacrifice into the dead vessel. QED.

And although the involvement of demons was nothing more than pageantry, intended to convince the magic practitioner that he had some idea of what he was doing, it allowed them to deduce the most likely victim. Whoever it was had chosen the Great Duke Saleos, which was a clue in its own right. Somehow an affair of the heart was involved. This was further backed up by Dame Holte's apparently irresistible fascination to otherwise respectable men.

It was clearly Jeb, therefore, who was the intended sacrifice. Who else was playing such a large part in the affairs of Hawkinge-By-Hythe's hearts? Who else was so inexplicably irresistible? "And what on Earth else," sniffed Gertrude, "could he be useful for?"

Colette sought out Jeb to enlist his help in unmasking the perpetrator, while Victoria visited Kelby, and Gertrude took care of the rest.

Chapter 9

A Big Dope Walks Into A Field

ON THE NIGHT OF THE 400TH anniversary, the three sisters were hiding in a copse of trees at the edge of Kelby's field together with Kelby and his son. The moon was up and apart from the discomfort of standing in long grass, which kept rustling in trepidation of the imminent influx of rats, it was almost pleasant. The night was cool but there was no breeze and the ground still radiated the day's heat.

Boots scraped along the road from Hawkinge-By-Hythe. "Just through here, dear." The woman's voice fluttered with excitement. From their hiding place the watchers saw Jeb with a large wickerwork basket, filled with feed from the corn chandler shop. He was stumbling along beside Mrs Sniffacre.

The rats could show up at any moment now that Jeb, the sacrifice, had arrived. Mrs Sniffacre continued to trudge towards them, holding Jeb's free arm and murmuring encouragement. He looked like a sleepwalker and let Mrs Sniffacre guide him to the middle of the field.

A big dope, was Gertrude's verdict, but she kept it to herself.

"Now!" shouted Colette.

Jeb dropped the basket, its paper bags of feed bursting. He ran towards the sisters. "She tried to poison me!" he said.

"Stop right there, Sniffacre!" Gertrude advanced from their hiding place with Kelby, who had his gun trained on Mrs Sniffacre, though not without misgivings. "This ends here," she said. "Do not call the rats!"

"Rats?" Mrs Sniffacre squealed and looked around. "Why would I –?"

"She came into the shop as we were closing and bought more feed. Offered me a drink when I helped her carry it home, but she put something in it." Jeb's eyes shone as he looked at Colette. "I watched what she was doing and played along, like you said."

"Rock sulphur!" said Mrs Sniffacre. "Just a little rock sulphur, so you'd walk out here with me. Carde always says how it keeps everyone nice and calm. I just wanted to come out for a walk with you, Jeb. We've been having lovely chats, but I knew you'd laugh, if I asked you to come out for a stroll, so I put a little rock sulphur in your gin, just so you wouldn't mind. I wouldn't harm you, Jeb!"

"And you just happened to be coming here? To the grave of Dame Holte?" Gertrude spat out the accusation. The Kelbys, father and son, each took a step back and gasped.

Mrs Sniffacre just nodded. "It's where we always come," she said.

Chapter 10

Here's Mud In Your Eye (Sockets)

"WE?" asked Victoria

"Any of the girls, who has a broken heart," she said. "Or a broken arm, after they're married." She paused. "Old Holte. I know it's wrong to say it, but she's almost like a patron saint to us. Oh, what she did was so wrong, but there's a peace in the field and sometimes it's good to come out and just talk. It's not like we're talking to the dead, she doesn't answer, but it can be good to get it off your chest when it's something no one wants to hear."

Victoria took Mrs Sniffacre's arm and moved with her away from the centre of the field. The poor old woman didn't know, but she was standing right over the dead body buried on the ley line and at any moment the rats would be back to conjure up the Rune of Re-Awakening for the final time. "My Ma used to bring me here when she'd come. I started coming again after my husband died." She covered her face. "Oh my God, I've made such a fool of myself!"

Instead of saying something like, "but you're old enough to be my mother!" Jeb patted her on the back and told her there was no need to be silly about things, and Gertrude's estimation of the young man rose slightly.

"Why would you need to bring him out here?" said Colette. She had always visited Jeb at home, where he had a shed at the back of the property, which he called his studio.

"I don't know, really. I get my confidence back when I'm here. I feel I have as much of a chance at love again as anyone." She stopped and covered her face again. After a sigh, she looked at them all. "I've bought more mash and feed than I could use in a lifetime."

"I'll ask Carde about his refund policy, if you like," said Jeb.

"Too late for that, dear. But thank you."

"What have you been doing with it?" said Gertrude.

"Just dumping it here," said Mrs Sniffacre. She gave Kelby a penitent look. "What else was I going to do with it?"

Jeb had picked up Mrs Sniffacre's basket, now he put it down again.

The sound of rustling reached them, and the sisters conferred quickly. Sniffacre wasn't behind it, she'd been duped into bringing the victim by someone else. "It's Holte," said Colette. "Has to be. The victim and the feed are just the bits she needed someone to do for her. It's Holte calling the rats. Controlling them."

"How?" asked Victoria.

"Ultrasound?" suggested Colette. "Female rats make high-pitched calls to attract males. If it's high enough and attractive enough, that might do it. Fool a few of the big bucks and the rest follow, hoping to get at the female, while the bucks fight it out amongst themselves."

"That would get them to the field, I suppose."

"If she can control her voice, make it sound like the female is moving, she can get the rats to follow it. Make them think she's always just in front of them. Race them around the field to draw the rune. Simple ventriloquism."

"You're not saying she's still alive?" said Gertrude.

"Unlikely after 400 years, I would say, but there's some sort of force still here amplified by the ley line. Call it a ghost or a spirit or a soul. Or just force of habit. Calling Mrs Sniffacre to bring a sacrifice. Calling the rats to conjure a demon she thinks will help her rise again."

"So she really was a witch, then?" said Kelby and immediately wished he hadn't.

"I don't get this," said Mrs Sniffacre. Like the Kelbys and Jeb, she had been unable to stop herself listening to what the sisters were saying. "She's four hundred years old. How could she rise again?"

Gertrude thought of the drawing. A figure clothed in rats. She shrugged. "Flesh is flesh. Kill Jeb for his energy, grab it when it flows to the ley line. Bind it before it can flow away again. Wear the rats as her skin."

Mrs Sniffacre fainted.

Jeb caught her and they all stood for an awkward moment, listening to the rustling approach. No one quite knew where to look. Jeb ignored everyone until Mrs Sniffacre's eyes fluttered open. She stood up quickly.

"Holte was going to kill me?" Jeb addressed the sisters and kept his voice level, though his face shone white in the moonlight.

"Yes, so don't worry, you'd have been dead before the really nasty stuff happened," said Gertrude. "I'll tell you what, though. You won't like this next bit." The sound of the rats had increased. Like Kelby had said, it sounded like the ocean. And it was almost upon them.

"Take Mrs Sniffacre home, would you, Jeb?" said Colette. Jeb and Mrs Sniffacre looked shy. "Up to you both, of course, but Holte has already called the rats. I'd advise you to leave before they get here." They hurried towards the road, not quite together, but not quite on their own either.

"That's your cue," said Victoria to the Kelbys. "Start harvesting. Cut as much as you can, starting with the rune. Before the rats arrive. Go!" Each of the sisters took a shovel and started digging in the centre of the field.

"It's impressive," said Gertrude. "A simple behaviour, grown powerful through repetition. You're right, Colette. Force of habit. Lasting four hundred years. She must have been an amazing woman, while she lived. A fascinating character."

"So they say," said Victoria.

"What do you intend, though?" said Colette. "We can't kill a habit."

"No," said Gertrude, "but we can weaken it, and then it can be broken. If we can dissipate enough of the influence, that should do the trick. Spread it out to get it away from the ley line, dilute its focus until it loses impetus." She paused. "Have they gone?" Mrs Sniffacre and Jeb were just disappearing out of view along the road.

"Poor thing!" said Victoria.

"This won't be pretty. Even a habit has to have something to cling to. Holte's bones are here. If we can scatter them..." The grave, which was located at the very centre of the rune, where the ley line bisected it, had been shallow and they had already reached the body of Dame Holte, exposing it to the air. There was not a bite of meat on her bones. The vertebrae in her neck looked undamaged: the hanging had been a short drop, with death caused by strangulation, rather than a snapped neck. "Or better yet..." Gertrude picked up the packets of mash that had been abandoned with the basket. Emptied it over the corpse and they dug around the skeleton, making sure it went everywhere. Over and under the bones. The soil had compacted around the remains, but Gertrude made sure she scooped it out from between the ribs and joints and eye sockets to replace it with feed.

Then the rats were upon them and they dashed back to their copse, joined by the Kelbys. The rats rushed towards the grave, then towards the edge of the circle. The bones of Holte had not noticed that they were finally laid bare to the elements of the pleasant summer night. Could not notice. All that was left of "Dame Holte" was a single loop of outraged behaviour. The rats continued on their course.

It was impossible for two men to clear the field in the time which remained before the rats were upon them, but the first thing the sisters had done, was to prepare markings, poles with flags, which Gertrude had arranged and planted strategically around the field where the occult lines overlapped, to erase as many of the key points and connections of the sigil and the rune as possible. All the men had to do was to hack away the crop at each of these spots. Without these key points, the sigil and rune remained fragmentary. There was no magic in an unfinished spell and no way for Holte or the rats to recognise that their task could not be completed. She released the rats, as before, when they had run their course. But this time they had noticed the food in the centre of the field and, exhausted by the run, they returned to it and ate their fill. They ate the feed together with everything nearby, including the skull and bones of the vengeful dead woman. Then they disappeared in every direction, dispersing the memory of bitter hate throughout the countryside in four-legged packets too small to do any damage on their own.

Chapter 11

All About Anatomy

THERE WAS A NOTICEABLE THAW in the air the next morning in the Alumière sisters' house. The previous night's teamwork had helped patch things up temporarily between Gertrude and Colette. It lasted until the evening when Colette arrived back with her camera, a parcel of developed photos and her top button once again conspicuously undone. It may still have been twenty-seven degrees and humid without a breeze, but Gertrude felt betrayed. After everything they'd been through and all they'd learned the previous night, Colette was still throwing herself at the silly young man.

"Who wants to see them?" said Colette.

"Pictures of the balloon adventure?" said Gertrude.

"Those too," said Colette. "It's not a toy, you know."

Birds twittered through the window, and Victoria sighed. "I'll go check on Curly, he's been quite pre-occupied the last few days."

"Here. Before you go," said Colette. "It's amazing the things you can do with a camera. Not only can you capture things for later, but there are all sorts of things you wouldn't otherwise notice. The camera puts them in a different light. And people behave differently, too. They can't help posing. Sometimes literally. It's fascinating." She handed the prints to Victoria. Gertrude poured herself a top-up from the teapot.

"Goodness!" said Victoria. "Yes, I see what you mean. I never would have known that he had a scar there otherwise."

"He wants to be an artist," said Colette. "But he wants to be a model, too. He knows all about anatomy and posing."

"I can see that!" said Victoria.

After a while Colette spoke again. "There's more than just that one photo, you know," she said. "Let me know when you've finished with it."

"Well, I rather like this one, to be honest." Victoria flicked to the next one. "Oh, you can see his face in this one. He's not shy, is he?"

"Anyway, I think I've got the hang of the camera now. And Jeb is heading off to London to seek his fortune, so there won't be any more ."

"Shame," said Victoria. Eventually she let Colette take the pictures back.

Colette placed the pile of glossy cards in front of Gertrude. Gertrude picked it up and glanced through them. She gave each one exactly thirty seconds before examining the next. Then she undid the top button on her blouse. "It is *hot* today, isn't it?" she said.

Colette sorted her photos into three piles. Those of Jeb, which she stored with her other "practice pictures," in a wooden box with the camera. Those of the rats and the sigil, which she tucked into an envelope with their case-notes on the matter. The third pile was of her balloon ride with Kaye. She had made copies of these when she developed the photos in the pantry of the apothecary's kitchen, which had been converted into a dark room. She would give one set to Kaye in the morning. She and Jerry had offered to take the three sisters for a private ascent the next weekend.

The heatwave had held the town in its grip for long enough. The weather was due to continue fine for the rest of the month, but the following Saturday was when the heat would finally break. The Alumières noticed the change in the atmosphere as they closed up shop in the early afternoon. Kelby had arranged for the balloon to be set up in his field to thank them for their help. Kaye and Jerry didn't want to draw a crowd for the moment, not until the newspaper had printed the photos of the heroic landing, which was to be part of their stunt repertoire in future.

They met Mrs Sniffacre as they headed towards Kelby's field. They saw her figure in the distance as they walked out of town. Saw how she slowed and stopped, standing in the road, having just realised that there would be no more "chats" with Dame Holte. So, they invited her to walk with them.

"I never thought it was evil," said Mrs Sniffacre after the topic of the weather had been exhausted. "None of us did."

"Nothing wrong with wanting to talk," said Victoria.

"And Tabby used to go there all the time, so it seemed alright."

"Tabby?" said Gertrude.

"Oh, before you girls came here. Tabby Mills. She's Mrs Gresstart now. The reverend's wife."

"*Really?*" said Gertrude.

"She had a hard life growing up. Lot of trouble. Had to stop coming after she married. The reverend found out she was visiting the old..." She thought for a minute to find the best word. "*Widow.* He was furious and put a stop to it. Well, because of his position, I suppose. Tabby would have been happy to keep coming, I dare say." Mrs Sniffacre's mood darkened. Here was someone else who seemed not to trust the reverend. "But I don't like to gossip. Oh, my!" She was getting out of breath as they climbed the hill.

"You're welcome to join us if you like," said Colette. "A quick spin in a hot-air balloon?"

"No-o. No, I think I need to keep my feet firmly on the ground from now on." She gave them a thin smile and a wave as she turned back.

"So that's why Gresstart got so worked up about the rats, but kept it to himself where they were going," said Victoria.

"Didn't know who was in on it. Didn't know who to trust. The price of paranoia," said Gertrude.

"'He sees his little Devils everywhere,'" said Colette, quoting De Glube.

Once again Jerry was left on the ground, as they couldn't all fit in the basket. Colette promised to take a few photos of him when they returned. "But don't let her talk you into anything you feel uncomfortable with," said Victoria, giving him an appraising stare.

It felt as liberating as before for Colette, and she could see from her sisters' faces that they were having the same experience. The balloon was tethered to its stump for their ascent. The sharp end of it was driven into the ground where Dame Holte's corpse had lain until very recently. Kaye had had to promise Jerry that she was unarmed before they lifted off.

In the distance, a motorcar sputtered its way through the winding country roads. A dark front of clouds was gathering to the west, but far enough away to be of little consequence to them. France had hidden itself on the horizon, and the sea and sky had blurred into a single blue-grey surface. A breeze tugged at the balloon and they swayed with it. It was followed by the scent of fresh-cut hay. "It's a beautiful part of the country," said Kaye.

"It does look beautiful," said Gertrude. Only Victoria and Colette heard the implicit *but*...

There was a procession coming towards them. Not rats this time. At its head a gaudy figure, surrounded by the muted browns of hand-me-downs.

"The professor," said Colette. The procession reached Mrs Sniffacre, still making her way back to town.

They couldn't hear what was being said, but there was a sudden burst of silver in the air and the children scattered – the professor had tossed a handful of sixpences into a field. The children dashed after them and he offered Mrs Sniffacre his arm. The sisters watched them disappear towards Hawkinge-By-Hythe.

The company would do Mrs Sniffacre good and there is no accounting for taste (as the professor's leg-wear demonstrated). Nonetheless, the sisters would be watching him. A friend of the reverend and an interest in mathematician, astronomer and alchemist John Dee? Very mysterious. Luckily, the sisters liked mysteries.

That would make a fine one for another day.

Acknowledgements

A huge thank you to my wonderful long-suffering wife, who has to put up with me *and* read all of my stories *and* provide feedback. Thank you! Mwah!

Thanks, too, to Siggi, my other "number one fan," as well as everyone else who has provided support and encouragement along the way.

Thank you to the Two Marks (Stay and Desvaux) who moderate the Bestseller Experiment podcast (Listen! Like! Subscribe!) and the related Bestseller Experiment Facebook Group. Thanks also to the members of the aforementioned Group, one of the nicest and most helpful writing groups on the planet (does the internet count as "on the planet?"). In particular, thank yous go to J. M. Carr for beta-reading and coining the phrase "cosy horror," and to Anne Woodward for beta-reading and suggesting I try culottes!

And to the amazing Claire Rushbrook, without whose world-class editing you would still be battling your way through the first chapter's commas: thank you!

About the Author

Morgan Delaney is an Irish writer of dark and fantastic fiction. Like all the great Irish writers, Morgan prefers to live abroad where there is less rain. "My pages stay dry and the ink doesn't run," he explains.

He has lived in Ireland, Germany, Australia and Kazakhstan, where he worked, among other things, as a building engineer. But one day, while he was writing a particularly outrageous cost estimate, the wind changed.

And he has been stuck like that—writing lies—ever since.

His favourite film is Terry Gilliam's Brazil.

Hawkinge-By-Hythe wants YOU!

When a demon takes over the body of a two-headed calf... it's time for the Alumières to fetch the heavy-duty rubber gloves.

"The Devil Rode Out"

When you sign up to Morgan Delaney's newsletter, you'll receive the Alumière sisters' very first adventure FREE!

You'll also receive a weekly email with stories, tips, reviews... and all the latest news from Hawkinge-By-Hythe.

"The Devil Rode Out" is available EXCLUSIVELY to subscribers. Discover Curly's origin story now!

(https://morgandelaney.info/newsletter/)

Also By Morgan Delaney

From humourous low fantasy to pitch-black horror!

Light Fantasy

The Alumière Sisters' Adventures

The Devil Rode Out (a subscriber exclusive)

The Phoenix

The Squared Circle

Darker and Stranger

People Skins. Dark, Strange and Fantastic Stories

People Skins, Volume 0: Hidden Cuts (a subscriber exclusive)

People Skins, Volume 1

People Skins, Volume 2

Pure Horror

Short, Sharp Horror Shocks

Sour Milk

Quick Deaths

www.ingramcontent.com/pod-product-compliance
Lightning Source LLC
LaVergne TN
LVHW091341190726
843491LV00002B/830

* 9 7 8 3 9 8 5 6 6 0 0 0 1 *